THE HAUNTING OF KNOLL HOUSE

by
CAT KNIGHT

VIDORRA HOUSE

©Copyright 2017 Cat Knight
All Rights Reserved

License Notes

This Book is licensed for personal enjoyment only. It may not be resold. No part of this work may be reproduced in any form or by any electronic or mechanical means including information storage and retrieval systems, without written permission from the author.

Disclaimer

This story is a work of fiction any resemblance to people is purely coincidence. All places, names, events, businesses, etc. are used in a fictional manner. All characters are from the imagination of the author.

CAT KNIGT

Table of Contents

Prologue 1

Chapter One - The Withered Town 9

Chapter Two - The Punishing 13

Chapter Three - The Dawn Walk 27

Chapter Four - Lady of the House 35

Chapter Five - Doll House Terror..41

Chapter Six - Torn and Tattered Images................................45

Chapter Seven - Through the Window..................................51

Chapter Eight - Beyond the Door 59

Chapter Nine - The Power of Mother....................................65

Chapter Ten - The Return of Sarah..69

Here is Your Preview of The Haunting of Stone Street Cemetery 74

   Chapter One - The Cemetery..75

   Chapter Two - The Consequence......................................87

Here is Your Preview of The Haunting of Highcliff Hall 92

   Prologue 93

   Chapter One - The Hag's Prophecy...................................97

Other Titles by Cat Knight..105

About the Author 106

CAT KNIGT

Prologue

Knoll House
South Downs
West Sussex
United Kingdom
August 1992

Claire didn't believe the rumours, and she didn't see why anyone else should either. She rolled her eyes at the gasps she got when she told people what she was planning to do, and their warnings just made her more determined. At least, until Sarah refused to join her.

"You can't be serious," Claire said. They were sitting on Sarah's bed and Sarah was playing with a doll while avoiding Claire's eyes, both of which struck her as very childish – eleven was far too old for that sort of behaviour.

"You know what they say," Sarah said.

"I know the scary stories our parents use to keep us away from the place."

"Maybe there's a reason they want to keep us away."

"They probably just think it's unsafe because it's old and rickety. As if we can't take care of ourselves. Come on; imagine the looks on everyone's faces when we tell them what we did."

"I just don't think that's worth dying," Sarah said, now twisting the doll's hair especially roughly.

"Are you scared?"

"Yes."

"You do realise there's no such thing as ghosts?"

"Well I don't realise that because I've never seen a ghost so how would I know for sure?"

"Listen." Claire grabbed the doll and threw it on the floor, which made Sarah finally meet her eyes. "All the boys who say that we can't join in with them will have to shut their fat mouths when they find out what we did. When school starts we'll be *legends*. And we don't have to tell them when we find nothing – we can come up with all kinds of crazy stories about what happened in there. I mean, obviously we'll have to get them straight together so it all matches up and people believe us, but it's totally worth it. And I won't have anyone saying that Claire Anderson backs down from a dare. Never have, never will."

"That does not seem like a smart way to live your life" Sarah said parroting something her parents often said. "What if somebody dared you to jump off a cliff?"

Claire ignored this.

"Sarah, you didn't see the look on Dave's stupid face. He *wants* us to back out."

"*I* want us to back out," Sarah retorted. "And I never agreed to it so it wouldn't even be backing out anyway."

Technically Claire did not agree with that – given that she had already said Sarah would do it.

But that was an unimportant detail. "Please Sarah?" she said. "Do it for me. We go in, we take a few photos, we get out. What's–"

"Don't say 'what's the worst that could happen'," Sarah said. "Whenever people say that the worst *does* happen."

"Sarah," Claire leaned forward. "It'll be fine. There is no such thing as ghosts. In, out, legends. I promise we don't have to stay long and I *promise* it'll be worth it."

Sarah bit her lip. Claire had to smile at that. She knew it meant she had won. They waited until past midnight, telling each other stories to keep awake until Sarah's parents had gone to bed.

When they were sure they were asleep, Claire and Sarah snuck into the kitchen where Sarah's mother kept her camera then, with one last nervous glance at each other, they walked out into the cold night and headed for the house Knoll House, up on the windy hill.

Claire had to admit, as each step took them slightly closer to their destination, that she *was* a little scared. She tried to remind herself that was illogical and stupid; old empty houses were just that – empty. But it was hard to argue with years and years of ghost stories, and rumours, about the old mansion on the hill.

She was pretty sure her parents had grown up scared of the place and her grandparents and probably every generation back to the last one who had lived there. But Claire believed in evidence. She had figured out Santa Claus wasn't real when she was three and she had never been the type to believe in anything she couldn't see with her own two eyes. It was that knowledge that made her push away every excuse.

It was too cold, they should wait until they had a better way of proving it, they should bring more people just so nobody could argue with what they had done. It would be so easy to find a reason to turn back and Sarah would agree without hesitation and despite promising that they definitely *would* go in the house at some point they'd probably never say another word about it and laugh at how silly and scared they were in ten years' time.

But that was the thing; that which separated Claire from generations of scared kids was a bull-headed determination. It made her keep walking, even as every shadow cast by a tree or streetlight started to look like skeletal arms reaching for them and the half-moon vanished behind lazily drifting dark clouds. The streetlights became sparser as they left the central part of the village and soon they were on the long, country road fringed with overgrown fields behind fences, the part of the village everyone liked to pretend didn't exist.

Any time she glanced at Sarah she could see, even in the darkness, how pale and terrified her friend was, and so she stopped glancing and locked her eyes on the road ahead. A couple of times she thought she saw Sarah, out of the corner of her eye, turn to her, mouth open, ready to ask if they could turn back. Maybe part of her wanted that to happen.

But Sarah never did and so they kept walking as the whistling wind picked up and the road slowly began to slope upwards.

A chill that had nothing to do with the weather came over Claire as she saw, in the distance at the top of the ever-steepening hill, the shape of the house. Why somebody every would have designed something so horrid, Claire couldn't say. Even in its prime it must have looked somewhat like an elongated skull.

Narrow windows overhung the dark maw of its veranda, the pillars seemed to hold it up like leering teeth, the only thing between them and the darkness beyond. Now the wood and stone were worn and grey, where once they had been painted brilliant white – something Claire was fairly sure could only have worsened the skull likeness.

A towering fence surrounded the house, but the hill meant that you could still see the whole bulk of it even from a distance, jutting up from the weeds and tangle of unkempt bushes that nobody ever did anything about. Over the years her parents had spoken idly of people who wanted to buy the place and fix it up, turn it into a bed and breakfast or the like, but that never seemed to happen. When Claire had been very small the almost permanent 'For Sale' sign that sat on the side of the road had been removed because, really, after so long what was the point anymore?

The best thing for the place would have been a visit from the wreckers, but nobody in this village could be bothered to go to those lengths, or maybe they were too scared to, and so Knoll House remained, terrifying everyone with the lingering belief that there was something inside you didn't want to disturb. Until tonight.

Feet from the fence, Claire and Sarah came to a halt. Claire's eyes scanned the distant building, focusing on the shape of it so as to keep her attention on anything but her beating heart. Beside her Sarah hugged herself, not saying anything. They must have stood there for at least ten minutes; both wanting to leave, neither wanting to say it.

But Claire had made a promise to herself and she was not going to give up on that.

In under an hour they would be on their way back home, victorious, with a camera that proved there was nothing inside but cobwebs and dust. Then finally everyone could shut up about the haunted house and finally, maybe, the boys would let Claire join in their games.

"Are you ready?" Claire whispered.

Sarah didn't reply. Worried that looking at her would weaken her resolve, Claire decided to take her silence as a yes and so she started to walk. For a few seconds, she heard nothing behind her and worried that Sarah might refuse to come after all – what she would do in *that* situation she couldn't say – but then she heard footsteps and together they headed for a famous gap in the fence, one people tended to come up and look through but never enter.

She felt short of breath already and her heart was growing louder by the second, but passing the first threshold that was the gap seemed to have ignited a tiny flame of courage in her heart, a flame that let her smile knowing she was already braver than just about every kid who had ever tried to take this challenge.

She turned to share her smile with Sarah, but one look at her friend's face made it clear that smiling was not on the agenda for her. Fair enough.

They kept walking.

The wind was picking up with every step, the dead trees and sprawling bushes rustling and shaking with increasing violence. Had Claire been more imaginative she almost could have fancied the sounds forming a voice. Go back, it said. Go back now before it's too late. She laughed quietly and shakily. She *was not* scared.

'Go back'.

The voice was as clear as day, from right behind her. She spun, but Sarah was still walking, head down.

"Did you say something?" Claire had to try hard to keep the tremor out of her voice.

Sarah shook her head. "Please don't try to scare me," she said. "Let's just get this over with."

Claire's eyes moved past Sarah, but all she saw were the bushes and the weeds. She made to turn.

'Please.'

She spun again. Sarah had passed her now and the voice had definitely come from behind, pleading and desperate. It sounded like somebody who would do anything to stop this moment from happened. It sounded like the stupid fear Claire had pushed away since she was a kid, the fear that made her want to cry out for her parents every time she had an ugly nightmare, the fear that tried to drag her down and tell her she was just another weak little child.

No.

Claire refused to entertain stupid fantasies a second longer. She turned her attention fully to the house now, which loomed up above them, dark and shadowy and more like a skull now than ever. She let herself feel that fear then she put it away in a little box, locked it and threw away the key. No more.

She picked up her pace, passing Sarah and climbing the front stairs on to the veranda. Rotting wood creaked and gave way slightly beneath her feet.

If that voice came again she couldn't say – she pushed everything away, everything except for the house.

She reached out and grabbed the rusted doorknob. It was ice cold. She looked back. Sarah had not come on to the veranda yet. She was frozen in front of the house, staring up at Claire, tears in her eyes.

For a moment they just stood there, looking at each other, as if a silent conversation was playing out. Claire turned the doorknob.

"Claire," Sarah said. Her voice was high pitched and cracking.

Claire paused.

"Please," Sarah said. "Please let's go home."

Claire pushed the door open and walked inside.

Chapter One - The Withered Town

London
United Kingdom
December 2017

She had gotten very drunk the night before; sitting by herself in a bar, knocking back whiskey after whiskey until she was kicked out and had to stagger home through the London streets. When her alarm went off that morning she wanted to smash it with a hammer, but even through her pain she knew that anger was more directed at herself than anyone else. She had known she had an early start that day. Had known it for weeks now. But still, drinking was the only way she was going to get any sleep that night. It had been the only way she could sleep for days now, ever since she had made this decision.

She arrived at the station early, dragging her case behind her. After picking up her ticket she tried and failed to choke down a sandwich, before spending ten minutes in the bathroom wondering if she was going to throw up. That sensation, she knew, probably had little to do with the hangover.

In the train windows, her reflection looked drawn and gaunt against the turbulent grey sky beyond.

Older than her twenty-six years. Although she had looked older than her years for a very long time now. Felt it too.

She tried to relax but knowing her destination made the journey impossible to enjoy. Simultaneously she wanted it to last for ever and end quickly. Every slowly passing second was a tightening screw, albeit one that brought her closer to the things she had been running from for more than half of her life.

She dreaded the moment the landscape became familiar. The fields, orchards and rivers that surrounded the village where she had grown up had soured over the years; even the best memories curdling like off milk as the moment that had been the dividing line between then and now infected all of them.

A slow cancer, moving outwards from the nexus point of one stupid, childish choice.

She leant her forehead against the cool glass and closed her eyes. It soothed her pounding head somewhat, although maybe that wasn't what she wanted. Maybe the real reason she had gotten so drunk last night, and the reason for all of those other nights and all of the other stupid things she had done, was the vague sense that she deserved it.

Was that masochistic, or just the smallest, most pathetic attempt to balance things out again? She supposed it didn't matter now. She opened her eyes and forced herself to watch the landscape change.

Maybe she should have given London a grander goodbye.

The city had been her home for a very long time after all. She had worked, studied, loved and lost there, made friends and planned a career all while that weight kept pulling her down until finally she had to roll the dice that would either cut it off for good or allow her to finally succumb to it. She wasn't even sure what she wanted more.

But, as the train moved, she knew that what really terrified her wasn't the ultimate destination of her trip.

It was everything that would come before that. Everything she had long since convinced herself she had escaped. The pointing fingers and accusing eyes, the forced smiles that tried to cover for all that hate and blame. Feeling like you deserved something did little to make you want to face up to *that*.

She had been on this train for a while now but the dread of familiarity had yet to shift into the awareness of it. She would have thought she'd have recognised the landscape by now. Or at least remember it from previous trips, because it was surprising that she could forget *this*. The grass was almost all dead in all directions, the orchards sparse and sad, bare tree branches reaching towards the grey sky as if begging for help. But not even the threatened rain could help this land. It looked dead and decayed, a long way from the green fields she knew so well.

But then...

She frowned. Something about the way those sad orchards lined up, the hills behind them and the placement of the fences *was* familiar, like a grey sketch of a famous painting. And that small cluster of houses looked a lot like the farm that marked the outskirts of her village and...

And in that moment Claire knew. She *was* home, and home was worse than she had dared suspect. The rot, it seemed, had not just permeated her life. As the train pulled into the village proper and she took in all those sights she had once known so well, a deep, hollow sadness took the place of niggling fear. Once this village had been vibrant, pretty and somewhat quaint – the perfect place to retire or bring up your kids, the kind of English village that adorned postcards. Now it looked as though all the colour had been sucked out of it, taking with it the life.

The paint was faded, bricks were cracked and worn, streets uneven. Looking at it all framed against the grey sky it was hard to imagine that the sun ever shone here. Around her, other passengers had stopped looking out the windows, returning their eyes to their phones and books and newspapers, turning away because they *could* turn away from the bad place, could ignore this terrible feeling of *wrongness* and go on to their destination with only the barest prickle of an uncomfortable memory. They did not need to call this void home. They did not need to come back here to right a terrible wrong.

As the train pulled to a halt and she gathered her things, she wished with such acute pain that she could be one of these simple ignorant people, averting her eyes until the land was pleasant and the world made sense again. To be protected from the pain by those thick glass windows. She wasn't sure she had ever been so jealous of anyone. She had dressed warmly but the cold still bit to her skin as she stepped on to the otherwise empty platform. She ignored her momentary desire to jump back on to the train and stay there until she was far away from here. The moment to turn away was gone and there was no point regretting it. Claire Anderson was home.

Chapter Two - The Punishing

Arundel
South Downs
West Sussex
United Kingdom
December 2017

When she was a kid the streets of the village would be bustling at this time of day. Neighbours stopping for a chat, impromptu coffee dates, kids playing openly in the grassy central strip; that vibrant sense of community that made you know that this was where you belonged, that here was safety and warmth and love.

She saw barely anyone now, as she walked up the footpath, half the shops she had gone into with parents and friends growing up were closed.

The ones that were open were largely empty; shelves poorly stocked and attendants sitting at their desks staring blankly at nothing. With colour had gone life; energy and passion drained away until nobody even had the wherewithal to just leave and go somewhere brighter.

She had thought that over the years her guilt had faded away to just a dull throb, always there in the back of her mind but never dragging her down or overcoming her like it used to.

That had been part of the reason she had chosen to return now, because it was the first time she had felt like she could really face the village. But seeing it all again brought that feeling back, growing larger and uglier with every step, that horrible twisted up sense of hateful wrongness inside that made Claire wish she had stayed on that train and just kept going until she was far away from all of this.

She hadn't even realised she was outside the bakery until she saw the old sign; faded now but with the same image as ever hanging above the propped open door. Claire paused for a moment then walked inside.

Kev was one of those men who had always been old; tall and thin with a fringe of grey hair behind his ears and the kind of bushy moustache that seemed to be designed to mock his pate. Nonetheless he always been like a favourite uncle to the kids of the village. Famous for his amazing milkshakes and patience for deluges of after-schoolers descending on his bakery and barely buying a thing.

Their parents used to tell them to stay away and leave him alone, but Kev didn't seem to mind and so the kids never stopped visiting. Like all the other shops there were no customers. Kev, looking the same as ever, moved around behind the counter, polishing things in his leisurely way.

He stopped upon hearing someone enter and then he turned. Claire, watched his eyes go wide and for a second Claire wondered if this had been a stupid mistake.

Despite the weirdness of the village, she was flooded with happiness when his face split into the familiar grin, a grin that not even the terrible rot that had claimed this place could destroy.

"Am I hallucinating?" he said.

"You're not that lucky," Claire replied with a smile, as Kev rounded the counter and embraced her. They stayed like that for a moment before Kev let her go and took a step back, looking her up and down.

"Skinny," he said. "You need some fattening. Milkshake, extra syrup?"

"I could think of nothing better," Claire said, muscle memory directing her to a nearby seat as Kev got to work, asking as he did how she was, what she had been doing, how the city had treated her but never once asking what had kept her away or brought her back. Some questions didn't need to be answered.

"How are you?" Claire cut him off mid-stream.

He faltered momentarily, glancing back at her. "Fine, fine," he said. "You know how small villages are. Nothing ever changes."

Claire glanced out the door behind her. "I don't know how true that is."

Kev followed her gaze. For a moment he just stood, staring out into the grey day. Then he shrugged and got back to work. "I suppose," he said. "When you live here it's incremental. Things shift so slowly that you have no idea it's happening until it's all ancient history. Must seem different to you."

Claire nodded. "But not surprising. It's worse than I thought, but I knew things would be bad." Kev finished the milkshake and brought it round. He sat as he passed it to Claire and for a moment neither spoke as she sipped.

It was bittersweet – the taste of a memory she'd thought long dead. A memory part of her had hoped was dead.

"You don't look well," Kev said. It was neither patronising nor concerned. Just a statement of fact.

"What did you expect?" Claire said.

"Didn't expect much, but I did hope," Kev said.

"Hope what?"

His smile was sad. "That'd you'd moved on.'"

The silence that hung over the table was no longer comfortable. Claire kept her eyes on her drink. "How could I?" she said.

"What happened wasn't your fault."

"I appreciate it, but that doesn't make you right."

"You've always been too hard on yourself."

"Funny, the rest of the village didn't think that," Claire said. "I felt like I was never hard enough."

"They are stupid and narrow minded." Kev's voice had more bite than Claire had ever heard there before. "They live in their little bubbles because they like everything just so and when something happens that challenges that they try to drive it away."

"I can't blame them," Claire said. "It was a big something."

"And you were *eleven*," Kev said. "You were a couple of kids doing what kids have always done and there was no way you could have known how it was going to go. No way *any* of us could have known."

Claire met his gaze and was surprised to see tears there. All of her own had long since dried up.

"There were rumours, weren't there?" Claire said. "For years, all that talk. I thought I was so damn smart. Proved myself very wrong there."

"Stupid kids don't deserve to be punished for being stupid kids," Kev said. "Even when they grow up to be stupid adults. Why are you here, Claire?"

She couldn't meet his eyes now.

"Just visiting."

"Rubbish."

"Haven't been back since I left. Figured it was time."

"That's a lovely story. What's the true one?"

She looked back out the door. "I want to put things right."

Kev leaned forward.

"You went through as much — more than the rest of them. Not only did you lose your best friend, not only were you there when it happened, but you came out of there only to be blamed for all of it for the next few years. Who are you putting things right for Claire? For the people who turned on an eleven-year-old girl who had just been through a trauma they could barely understand?"

"There was more to it than that and you know it," Claire said. "I don't love how I was treated Kev, but I *get* it. What happened to Sarah was my fault. If I hadn't pushed her into it, if I hadn't insisted we go in that house even though… even though I…"

That old dizziness – that feeling of her head swimming and her heart starting to race as something prickled in her eyes – was back. She knew this feeling.

She hated this feeling. She tried to stand but was shaking too badly. She closed her eyes and took several long, deep breaths. When she opened them, Kev was watching her steadily.

"It's time to let go," Kev said.

"I agree."

"Then what are you doing here?"

"Letting go."

"How?"

Claire looked away.

"They won't forgive you," Kev said. "They're too twisted up. So how…" he trailed off. When he spoke again his voice was quiet. "You can't."

"It's the only way," Claire said.

"It's suicidal."

"I have to try."

Kev grabbed her hand. "No, you absolutely do not. Sarah is gone, Claire. There's no other way around it. She's gone and she's not coming back and nothing you do will change that, not for you or her parents or anyone."

"I can bring them closure," Claire said.

"*Nothing* will fix what they lost."

"But saying goodbye might help them," Claire said. "I owe them that much, Kev. I owe this *village* that much." Tears were running down Kev's cheeks now. He wiped them off.

"This village eradicated any debt you had by making you a pariah. I won't see you die for them."

Claire got to her feet. "It won't be for them," she said. Then she turned and walked back out on to the street.

She took a few moments to compose herself, before continuing on her way. As she did the wind picked up, turning from a moan into a howl that moved between the streets, coming from a direction she knew all too well, a direction she had looked in countless times over the years that had finally brought her to this moment.

Soon.

She saw a few more people as she walked, leaving the main street and entering the blocks of houses. Some ignored her. Others stopped and stared as she passed – usually the ones she recognised. She didn't insult them or herself by smiling or waving. She wasn't wasting her time on false pleasantries.

It was harder to ignore the yells, when they came. Little old Mrs Shannon, somehow still alive, screaming *murderer* from her front porch, trying to get up and hobble towards her. Rotund Mr Herbert telling her to go back where she came from. Hearing that stung. Part of her had hoped things would have changed, but she had heard it all before and with more venom and anger.

After so many years it felt like a tired reflex, an action taken more because they didn't know what else to do than out of any real fury. The memory of an emotion rather than the thing itself.

Being back brought back many feelings but, as she got closer and closer to the house she had grown up in, fear, anger and guilt were slowly outweighed by a deep, aching sadness.

She had not told her parents she would be back; they would have begged her to stay away, and while she was sure they would welcome her she wasn't sure she was ready for what would follow. The averted eyes, the silent dinners, the feeble attempts at cheeriness always tempered by the never-ending desire to press her. The patterns she had gone through day after day until that blessed moment she could leave. What happened in the house? What she had done? Whose fault it really was.

Her silence had confused and frustrated them even as it slowly turned their family into one the village blamed and avoided. Most kids never had to learn that love was seldom unconditional, that there were boundaries to what a parent could deal with. Claire supposed it had been a valuable lesson, but that didn't mean it was one she had ever appreciated having to learn.

Like everything else here, the house looked like a washed-out facsimile of the one she had known; all the parts the same, but somehow just... *less*. She had been so proud of it as a kid, of its size and beauty and the explosion of colours that made up their garden. She could never imagine wanting to live anywhere else. For a long time since she had struggled to imagine setting foot inside again.

But here she was, standing at the end of the long sloping driveway, looking up at the front door she had run through so many times; and trying to muster up the courage to knock and ask for permission to enter her own home.

Perhaps she should have been upset by this. But then she supposed Kev was right about incremental changes. It was very easy to get used to pain when it started small and worsened slowly. She took her time walking up the garden path, letting her eyes move over it all.

The bushes, the grass, the cobblestones beneath her feet, the broken old birdbath that nobody had ever gotten around to fixing, all remained as they were, yet somehow, more broken.

She took in everything because she had not seen any of it in years, she may never see it again, and it delayed the moment of having to knock.

But that moment arrived, in that way all moments you attempt to delay do; far too soon. She stared at the wooden door and tried to muster courage that seemed to have fled. She raised her hand, then dropped it again. She clenched and unclenched her fists. Then, moving fast as if she was tearing off a band aid, she knocked. For a moment, she heard nothing and it was very close to a relief. Then the footsteps; slow and shuffling. She moved back as the door opened and her father took her in for the first time in eight years.

Claire went to speak but everything she had planned and rehearsed was gone. Her father's eyes were wide, his mouth opening and closing. Then he stepped forward and hugged her and she hugged him back and wished she wasn't crying.

She didn't know how long they stood like that. When her father finally let go and stepped back there were tears in his eyes as well and despite everything Claire knew she was smiling.

"Come in," he said, voice hoarse.

She followed him through the front hall, looking around as she did at the photos and paintings on the wall, none changed or moved. Together they walked into the living room. The TV was playing and her mother sat watching.

"Who was that?" she said, without looking back.

"Hi Mum," Claire said. Her mother seemed to stiffen. Then, slowly, she turned. Her hair was greyer and her face thinner than Claire remembered, but otherwise familiarity hit her like a punch to the gut.

"Claire," she said.

Her mother stood slowly. Her expression was wary. "What are you doing here?"

"It's still my home. Isn't it?" Claire asked, a little more defensive than she'd planned.

"But you..." her mother seemed lost for words. "It's been years. We haven't heard from you in..."

"A long time," Claire said. "I'm sorry."

Her mother nodded. Her mouth twitched slightly, a smile or something else fighting against her always consummate control. She stepped forward. Then the smile won and they were hugging as well. For the first time since she had stepped off that train, maybe for the first time in years, Claire remembered what home had felt like.

And then old routines took over. Her father set about making tea while her mother grilled her with questions; where was she living, where was she working, was she eating alright, did she have a boyfriend – the questions came thick and fast.

For her part, Claire was just happy for this tiny, brief glimpse of normality, of a life that had not been eaten from the inside out by something that none of them had ever really understood.

She sat and drank tea after tea as they talked and it was only as dinner time neared that the first question, the biggest question returned.

"So why *are* you back?" her mother asked from her armchair. "You haven't set foot here in so long. What changed?"

Claire had planned several evasions and lies for this moment, but being here now, seeing them again made the futility of that clear. There was no point in lying when you might never see someone again. That, she now knew, was the time for honesty.

"I'm here to find Sarah's body," she said.

Her friend's name, so often a forbidden word in her teenage years, seemed to make the room colder and dim the lights. Her mother's mouth tightened and her father looked away.

"Why?" he said quietly.

"Because she's been in there long enough," Claire replied.

"People tried to find her," he said. "And–"

"I know," Claire said.

"And they died."

For the first time since arriving home Claire felt a surge of something like anger.

"Obviously I know that," she said. "Nobody ever let me forget it."

"Claire..." Her mother looked around, as if trying to find the words. "It's been... I think you might have forgotten. Having not been here. But that house is... there is something about it that we can't understand. Something evil. A lot of people tried to find Sarah after what happened. And then to find the ones who tried to find her. Nobody ever came out."

"*Somebody* came out," Claire said. "Me."

"Yes, you did," her father said. "And I know that we did a terrible job of making sure you knew this, but we were so, *so* grateful that you survived. Have you any idea how that felt? To see Sarah's parents, see what they were going through and to privately thank God that it was their child and not ours?"

"I don't Dad," Claire said. "But do *you* have any idea how it felt to walk out of that house and wish that you hadn't? Because God knows, this village spent a long time telling me that that was how *they* felt."

"What happened was unprecedented," her mother said. "Nobody knew how to act. They settled on cruelty and that was wrong. But you don't need to run in there chasing some kind of redemption."

"Actually, I think that's exactly what I need to do," Claire said. "That house was there for years and everyone knew it was bad, but the village was still fine, right? Everyone was happy, everything prospered."

She paused, remembering.

"After Sarah went in there, after I came out... well, you see it every day, don't you? That poison spreading. I think that when I walked out of that place and left Sarah in there, I took something with me. Something that settled on the village and has been destroying it ever since. And *that* makes me think that the only way to put an end to it, the only way that makes sense, is to go back in. If anybody stands a chance of surviving, it's me."

"You don't even remember how you did it last time," her father said. "Or at least, you say you don't."

There it was. That same tone she had heard so many times growing up. If it wasn't outright accusations, it was clumsy attempts to gauge whether she had been lying.

How could it be that she didn't remember anything? She had learned to forgive her parents for their doubt; she would have wondered herself, if she hadn't lived the amnesia. But it didn't make it any less frustrating.

"I say I don't because I don't," Claire said. "I get that... I get that a lot of people think I hurt Sarah. But I was nowhere near the house when the others disappeared. Anybody with half a brain knows there is something wrong about that place, but for some reason it didn't hurt me." *Not directly anyway.* "I owe it to Sarah, to this village, to go in there and find out why. Because if I really am the one who started this, then it stands to reason that I might be able to finish it."

Her parents looked at each other. There was a silent communication passing between them, she knew, some debate about what to say or if there even *was* anything to say.

"And what if you don't end it?" her mother said. "What if you make it worse?"

"Worse than what?" Claire said. "Think I can suffer more than I have in the past fifteen years? Think this village can lose any more of its life?" She shook her head. "The damage has been done. The only thing left is to see if it can be *undone*. And the only person who can do that is me." She stood. "It's been a long trip. I'm going to get some sleep."

"When?" her mother said. "When are you going to do this?"

Briefly, Claire considered lying. It might go some way towards stopping them trying to convince her not to. But then, she had made her choice and she knew nothing would change her mind now. "Tomorrow," she said, then turned and walked out of the room.

Chapter Three - The Dawn Walk

Her childhood bedroom was the same as it had ever been. Preserved, like the rest of the village and the house. But the life of something could never be retained along with the look of it, and so the room felt more like a graveyard, a sad monument to the girl she had been.

She sat up late that night, sifting through her old books and toys. She found a dusty diary from before she and Sarah had entered the house, and she lay there reading it for hours, laughing occasionally, pausing to fight back tears at other moments. The stories in here were so mundane – stories of boys and games, of fights with friends and the injustice of parental decisions.

With her teenage years so overshadowed by Sarah, it had been easy to forget that at some point she had been a real kid who lived a completely unremarkable life. It was funny how, looking back from the other side, the unremarkable could seem so very remarkable. Or at least it was funny until she remembered how sad it was.

Sarah was everywhere.

The name repeated in the diary again and again, the comic they had written together when they were eight, birthday cards with long, rambling, sincere messages that got harder to read as they filled the whole card and the writing had to become microscopic to fit.

The betrayal had never felt keener than in the moments when the depth of their friendship was remembered.

By the time Claire switched off the light and lay back on her bed she wondered if there was any chance of her sleeping tonight. It might be her last night alive and she was going to spend it tossing and turning. It made sense, but it seemed a shame, not to get to sleep one last time.

It was funny to think about everything she was saying goodbye to. Sleep. Food. Television. All those mundane things. She hoped she wouldn't have to say goodbye, she hoped that things would work out, but to make this choice she had to know that she was ready to face the consequences if she needed to. But being ready didn't mean she *wanted* to.

Kev had suggested what she was doing was suicidal, and maybe it was, but that didn't mean Claire was doing it out of any desire to end her own life. Because facing the end made you face realities, and one of the hardest ones to swallow was the growing realisation that she didn't really believe she deserved to die, no matter what everyone seemed to think.

Kev was right; she had been an eleven-year-old girl doing the kind of things that other eleven year old girls did all the time. Usually there wasn't any punishment. And that was the complicated thing; she was so, *so* angry at the way she had been treated by the people of this village, at the injustice of it.

But, she had also seen firsthand their pain. Claire had come to realise the horrible truth.

That grief makes monsters of the most reasonable people, and it takes a certain kind of patience to be able to swallow that.

Part of her wanted them all to suffer and rot here forever. Part of her thought that what she was doing now came from a place of steely pragmatism more than anything else.

Claire wanted to wrap up unfinished business, so that could move on. But below all the rationalisations and explanations the truth was simple. She knew she had to do this, and so she would do it.

At some point sleep claimed her. She woke up before dawn, still in her clothes, lying on top of the bed surrounded by her old books and papers. Outside the window it was still dark. Perfect. She got to her feet and took her time replacing everything, leaving the room as if nobody had ever disturbed its impeccable little monument.

Then she walked out into the hallway and down the stairs. She had almost reached the front door when her mother's voice stopped her.

"Claire."

She paused, briefly considered just hurrying on her way, then turned and walked into the living room. Her mother sat by herself in her usual armchair, wearing a dressing gown with a glass of wine in her hand. She looked as tired as Claire felt.

"Did you sleep?" Claire asked.

"No. Did you?"

"A little."

Her mother grimaced. "You are going to do this, aren't you? No matter what I say?"

Claire nodded.

"You know that..." Her mother faltered, closed her eyes, took a deep breath and fell silent.

Claire waited for her speak again. Her mother started again. "Claire. You know that we always loved you, no matter what. And we never... we never blamed you for what happened."

Claire hadn't known that. But it made no difference now.

"Those days were... strange and confusing," her mother went on. "None of us knew how to act and so none of us acted the right way. It's no excuse, but every day you've been gone I've been realising how much we messed up. And if you thinking you have to do this is our fault then..."

"It's not," Claire said.

"But if we had tried harder–"

"You did the best you knew how to do at the time," Claire said, not unkindly. "That's the best anyone can do. I don't blame you or Dad for any of it. I really don't."

They held each other's gaze for a long time. But Claire didn't walk over or hug her or anything else. She had prolonged the inevitable enough already.

"I love you Mum," Claire said. "Tell Dad the same." She walked out the front door and into the cool, dark morning.

Sometimes as a kid she had done the same; wandering her village before the sun came up or the people started to rise. Sometimes she had done it with Sarah but usually she was alone, doing something that belonged to her. It felt almost good to be here again.

But she had one more stop before her final one. A house she had avoided for years, a house she had not seen, let alone been inside, since the night this had all begun.

And walking to that house felt more like walking to the gallows than her last destination ever could.

But she held her head high as she approached Sarah's home and she let the memories wash over her and she knew that she had to do this. She was tired of waiting. So, she walked up to that front door the two of them had left through together so long ago and she knocked. She knocked again and again until the door opened and Sarah's bleary-eyed father was there, looking ready to yell but freezing when he saw who had disturbed him.

"I just wanted to say that I'm sorry," Claire said. "And that I'm about to go to that house and do everything in my power to find Sarah and bring her home."

She didn't need to hear the sneering or the attack or the slammed door. So, she just turned before Sarah's father had even had a chance to react and she walked. He was calling her name, again and again, telling her to come back but whether forgiveness or blame was his intent she didn't need to hear it. She just walked, taking in the dark again that same route from so long ago, leaving the village proper and reaching the long stretch of desolate road that led to the house on the hill.

As she walked alongside the fences she could almost imagine that Sarah was here, walking alongside her and telling her to go back, that they could lie or come up with some excuse or just take the inevitable jeering and move on with their lives. She should have listened then and she would have listened now but there was no-one there to listen to and so she just kept walking. And then there it was, distant but clear against the slow rising sun.

The house that she had always thought looked like a looming skull. Framed by blood red it seemed to be challenging her, taunting her.

You're back Claire Anderson. You couldn't beat me last time, what makes you think you can now?

She stopped. She had no reason to think she could. No reason at all. None but the barest sense of *maybe*. But that was more than she had had for years.

She kept walking making herself look at the house as she did. It seemed to be trying to force her to avert her eyes, to show due deference to the place that had ruined her life and claimed so many others.

But, perhaps absurdly, she wasn't going to give it that victory over her. Not when it may be about to get the biggest one. She just kept looking at it as it grew and grew until finally she was standing at the foot of that sickeningly familiar hill, entirely in the shadow now cast by the half-risen sun.

But she didn't pause. She walked up the hill and towards that old gap in the fence. It was a little more difficult than it used to be to get through, but she managed it.

Around her now was the tangle of overgrown garden no-one ever tended and the whisper of wind through it all. That voice she had once fancied was telling her to go back.

She ignored all of it.

Claire Anderson walked once more up to the house and on to the creaking, wooden porch. She stood in front of the peeling door and remembered the last time she had done this. The threshold she had crossed to the darkness that came after. She stood there and refused to look back or hesitate as she reached out, opened the door, and walked inside.

CAT KNIGHT

Chapter Four - Lady of the House

Knoll House
South Downs
West Sussex
United Kingdom
December 2017

A grey mist obscured her view, Claire took a tentative step forward when it happened, for an instant she felt she was falling.

But then, it was so wonderful, so very wonderful indeed. The sun was out and the day was beautiful and she could not wait for Edward to take her walking along the river while the children played on the grass. For once no work or school to drag them away. For once the company of her family, the way it was supposed to be, the way it had been before life put this stranglehold on them and eked away their happiness until—No. She wasn't to think about that. If she thought about that she might be sad and on this day of all days she could not allow herself to be sad.

Not where they might see her.

Because then Edward would worry and the children would ask what the matter was and somebody would suggest doing something else but she would beg them to go out nonetheless. And so, they would but it would all be so very tense and bitter and she did not want that. Not today. Not when everything was so very wonderful. So, she made herself smile in the mirror and when it didn't look real she hit herself then again and again until there were tears in her eyes but her smile was oh so wonderful.

The children would be so happy to see it. Then she ensured her clothes were immaculate. All the other husbands would look at Edward and be jealous; and then she walked out of her room and down those grand sweeping stairs to where her family waited, Edward at the door and the children in their Sunday best close by. Edward beamed at her and he opened the door and it was so wonderful but then someone was stepping through the door and–

Claire felt like she had been doused in ice cold water. She staggered and reached out a hand, finding soft mould and a layer of dust over it. Everything was dark. She fumbled for her bag, pulling out a torch and all the while wondering what the hell had just happened.

The moment she stepped through the door she had seen... well, she wasn't sure what she had seen. She had been, for a few seconds, someone else, but being in that person's head was like being jabbed by a thousand needles from every direction, over and over again, while trying to act like nothing was amiss.

Clair shook herself. It didn't matter now. Strange things happened in this house, and brief hallucinations were the least of her worries. She turned on the torch and looked at what was ahead of her.

It seemed familiar. She supposed she *had* been here before. But the familiarity was vague; more like a recurring dream you can never quite remember than somewhere she knew well. She was standing in a vast front hall.

Maybe once it had been opulent – in fact she was fairly certain now that it *had* been – but it was a ruin. The walls varied between grey and brown, claimed by mould, mildew and time.

The floorboards were broken in many places, with gaps into darkness below. It was cold in here; colder than the morning outside had been.

Despite the rising sun and the almost certain presence of gaps in the walls, there was no sign of natural light. All she had was the torch.

She turned and tried the doorknob behind her. It burned cold in her hand and half surprised her with a jolt as it refused to give way, locked now. Somehow, she had expected that. A thought tempted her to leave, but she was stuck in here now. Even if she wanted to leave she was going nowhere unless the house wanted her too.

The most likely conclusion was, that she wasn't leaving, probably ever. But the one Claire preferred draw was that there was a way and it was through this house. And, the house would not claim her as it hadn't before — she would leave with Sarah's body.

Raising her bag over her shoulder Claire started to walk, taking care to mind the gaps beneath her feet. Logically there wouldn't be anything but dirt and insects under there, but this place didn't operate on anything that could be construed as logic.

She paused at the foot of the stairs. They were placed centrally in the hall, and around either side were doorways. She figured the best option was to search every floor end to end and hope that enough memories would come back to her to tell her where she had last seen Sarah. Glancing from side to side, she then moved to the left, noticing a slightly ajar door in the shadow of the staircase.

As she observed it she heard a loud, unmistakeable creak from above her. Involuntarily, she held her breath. Her heart rate picked up and her skin prickled. *Was she alone in this house?*

She could not honestly know the answer to that question, short of being sure that this was not just an old wreck. But if there was another person in here, was the safer option to alert them to her presence or not?

She glanced behind her, at the locked front door. It wouldn't be a person and whatever it was knew she was here. There was no reason to call out then. No reason to invite whatever was surely coming.

Pushing onward she heard a snatch of what could only be high pitched laughter from above. Every instinct urged her to run for the locked door and beat on it, till it let her out; but her instincts meant nothing now. *The only way out is through.* She walked through the doorway. Claire found herself standing in a long hallway, stretching down into shadow and then—

—it was so wonderful how the children ran up and down, playing and shrieking and chasing each other, if only they could be a little quieter to let her headache pass but it was so wonderful... and why was she holding that knife—?

For the briefest second the space had been full of light. But now the dark was back. It seemed thicker, somehow. Or had she imagined that? Somehow, she didn't think so. Claire felt unsteady on her feet. One foot in front of the other, she started to walk, keeping the torch aloft.

She did not notice the door quietly swing shut behind her.

CAT KNIGHT

Chapter Five - Doll House Terror

There were a few doors along the hall. Careful to avoid the holes in the floor, Claire checked each one as she passed. The first opened into an empty room, as drab as desolate as the rest of the house. She left that and went to the next, where she found what seemed to be a children's play room. Old, moulding dolls lay about the floor and at the far end was a towering, elaborate, but decrepit dollhouse.

Claire walked in, scanning the walls with her torch as she did. It was clear there were no people in here, but she looked over all of it anyway. The dolls, with their wide staring eyes and straggly remnants of hair, gave her the creeps. But, for whatever reason, it was the house that fascinated her.

The closer the got, the more she realised what she was looking at. It was a perfect replica of the house she was in, down to the last detail. Somebody had crafted this with loving care. She reached out and touched it. It seemed reasonably sturdy, despite its destroyed appearance. She pulled it open and with the screech of a rusty hinge, the front swung out.

Inside it represented all the rooms that she assumed made up the house, upstairs and down.

Almost without thinking she found her current location and froze as she saw a small, wooden figurine standing there. The figure of a woman holding... she leaned closer. Yeah. That was definitely a torch.

Something was obscuring her face. She reached out a thumb to wipe it off and it came away sticky.

It was blood.

Above the figurine, the roof of the house was *bleeding*, dripping down on to her.

She got to her feet, turned around and was faced with someone in the doorway, someone in a dress, someone with a leering, skeletal face and thin hair dangling over it, someone who reached for her as she screamed and then–

And then was gone. The room was empty.

Claire shook uncontrollably. She called out, demanding to know who was there, but the house was silent. She glanced back at the house. The little doll was almost completely covered in blood now.

Her throat constricted and with her heart beating through her chest she hurried back out into the hall.

Outside the house, the sun would be almost fully risen by now, but there was no light. Even Claire's torch seemed to be struggling to penetrate the gloom; she could only see a few feet in front of her.

Fear of what was to come gripped her and she paused before opening the next door.

The blood and the figurine with the torch burned into her mind and she wasn't sure she was ready for whatever waited in the rest of the house. But then, ready didn't matter. Not in a situation like this.

Evil had been done here it had nothing to do with her. She pulled away, forced her heavy limbs to move, to run back the way she had come. She felt dirty, she felt contaminated and in the dark, all she saw was the blood.

She grabbed the door handle and tugged again and again but it didn't move. She turned and now the blood was leaking from the room.

Slowly, it covered the floor and dripped between missing floor boards as it spread. Terror gripped her as she hit the door and cried out in futile rage. The torch slipped in her grip as she pounded. Helplessly she watched as it rolled over the edge and went through a gap in the floor and suddenly she was in darkness, not knowing how close the blood was, and when it would reach her and what would happen when it did.

Claire knew what she needed to do. She must retrieve the torch. Tentatively, she took a step forward hearing only her own heavy breathing. Gathering her courage once more, Claire closed her eyes and lowered herself into the gap.

CAT KNIGHT

Chapter Six - Torn and Tattered Images

Claire expected to hit dirt or concrete. Instead her feet sunk down into something thick and gluttonous, something that, the deeper she went, she knew to be blood. How had it got so deep? The metallic smell filled the air and in moments her head was under. It was warm, but horribly so. It felt *alive*.

She tried to swim upwards but her arms moved so slowly through the thickness and although she kept her mouth closed tight it seeped through to her tongue. It was all over and around her, closing in and suffocating. Her lungs burned. She tried again to swim upwards, to get clear of it again, but her limbs had lost all their strength. Sinking deeper she felt everything recede; the terror, the inability to breathe, the need to escape.

Would this be so bad? To just let go here and slip away? She had tried, after all. She had suffered for so long and wasn't it better to die doing the right thing than to live doing nothing? Nobody could ever blame her for giving up now. She had been through more than most could ever imagine and she was just so damn tired.

Her limp hand touched something solid. *The torch.*

And then it was all there again, burning through the slow rot of acceptance; the memory of *why* she was here, of what she had to do and what she owed, because while death would end it for her, it would not for anyone else. And that meant she had to fight.

She grabbed a hold of the torch and, with every ounce of strength she had, muscles screaming and lungs an inferno, she forced herself up and up. She opened her mouth to cry out. It filled with blood but she ignored it. She had to ignore it because no matter what it *could not* be happening, this was a trick, a way to try and make her give up, an attempt by the house to win.

Her head broke the surface. The arm that held the torch followed then the other, reaching upwards and finding the jagged edge of one of the holes in the floor. She tossed the torch through, reached up her other arm and pulled.

Clearing the hole, she scrambled out, not caring that the broken wood was tearing her clothes and her skin, not caring about the pain because the pain meant that she was still alive and the house had not beaten her. Not yet.

She collapsed on to her side, taking deep breaths, letting herself shake and cry and feel it all but laughing because she was *alive* and that meant that she still had a chance of finding Sarah's body and getting out.

It took her a while to realise that something was odd. She was able to breathe fine. She sat up and, turning on the torch, looked down at her hands. She should be covered in sticky blood. The torch should be unable to work after that. But she was clean, if a little scratched up.

Standing up, she noticed something else, she had fallen through the hole in the hallway floor she was walking down. But somehow, she had emerged back in the front hall, through one of the other gaps in the floorboards. Shining the torch down through the length of the room, she again saw only darkness.

She moved the beam up over the stairs, to the landing at the top of the stairwell.

The house seemed to be in its prime and Claire thought she caught a glimpse of a woman. But, in an instant the woman disappeared. Claire felt the woman once more in her mind. She was coming to meet her husband and her children.

Before, when Claire had felt the woman she had put it aside and hoped that it was only her imagination. She was now certain she was something other than that.

Above her on the empty stairwell came a creak. Then another. And another. Claire shone the torch around, peering in the darkness. It sounded very much as though somebody was walking around up there. She knew what was required, she had to go up.

"Have it your way then," Claire whispered, and walked on towards the stairs.

The first step seemed to give way a little beneath her foot, then the second did the same, years of decay weakened them and they bent beneath her weight. She was careful to try and only stand on the parts that seemed the most stable. Gingerly she continued up, step after step until she stood on the landing.

And then, as if from right behind her, she heard the voice of young girl, somehow, intimately familiar.

"Come on Sarah, let's see what's upstairs!"

Claire spun. Her eyes moved back down the stairs and then along the hall again. Sweeping the old floors with her torch, she saw nothing. Just the decaying house, empty and still.

Closing her eyes, she breathed deeply to calm the thundering rush of blood that pumped through her veins. There was no doubt in what she had heard. Uncontrollable tremors shivered along her limbs. Whatever it was, or whoever she thought it might be would be waiting was at the other end of the hallway. It couldn't possibly be what she thought, but the house played by its own rules. She focussed her eyes forward again, looking at the large pair of double doors just beyond the top of the stairwell, and continued toward them.

One of them was slightly ajar. Claire grabbed and pulled it wide open, exposing another hall behind it, as dark and derelict as the rest of the place. This time, however, she moved the light of her torch over to the rusted hinge, the nails holding it loosely in place.

She put the torch between her teeth then pulled on the door hard; once, twice, three times until it came loose from its hinges and dropped to the floor. She almost tumbled back down the stairs but she had made sure the house wouldn't be locking her in here, in this space.

The hall opened up to several other passages, going in various directions. Claire followed it down, pausing now and again, trying to work out in her head how it matched with the house as it looked from the outside. The simple answer was, it didn't. The house was changing at its will, something she knew she probably should have suspected long ago.

Claire closed her eyes again. Something seemed to be tugging at the corner of her memory, something a tiny bit stronger than vague familiarity. She had been here before. The floor and the walls felt familiar. Just ahead of her, in an outline so faint that they might have been made out of mist.

If she really looked she could almost see two eleven-year-old girls moving cautiously through the halls.

Claire gasped in shock, wanting to trust herself, to call out to them and warn them because she felt their confidence was growing with each second. She wanted to tell them that they were wrong that there nothing in here and that they would be okay. Because they would not be OK.

A deepening mist seeped up from the floor and rolled along the corridor, Claire's heart raced, as the outline of the girls faded further into the fog. Moving frantically through the mist, the choice to believe in herself came instantly. She called out but they did not hear her. If she lost them, she feared they would be lost forever.

She could not let that happen. Now as they disappeared from view completely, Claire stopped. There was nothing else that she could do, but search the ever-changing rooms until the house gave up its secrets. So, with single minded effort, she chose a turn at random and followed it knowing that if the house sensed she was beating it, then the rug would be pulled from under her. She was therefore unsurprised to find that this time there were no doors lining the hall.

But there were frames, dozens and dozens of them. Damaged, emptied picture frames.

Most still displayed the torn edges of canvas that had been forcibly ripped out. Some held most of a painting, but where the faces of these serenely posing people should have been were only gaping black holes, as if someone had burned them out. She recognised the forms of some of them, those that had come before, those who had come searching for the body of Sarah, now a stark legacy to the village folk that had never returned.

She kept walking. Minutes passed and the hallways didn't end, nor did the ruined paintings.

Then, right when she was ready to turn and head back, she found a painting that was intact.

It caught her eye immediately; even from a distance, even not knowing was it showed, she felt a prickle on the back of her neck at the sight of it, some deep sense of terrible *wrongness*. Her hand tightening around the torch, she approached it.

It showed the house, stark against a turbulent grey sky. The land around it was overgrown and unkempt. This was not the place in its prime.

In front of the house was a tree, a tree Claire was fairly sure was not there in real life. And hanging from the tree—

She clapped a hand over her mouth to hold back the pained cry.

Chapter Seven - Through the Window

Hanging from the tree was Sarah. And standing below, placidly looking up at her, was Claire. Not eleven-year-old Claire, but Claire as she looked now.

She could not help the tears in her eyes, tears of sadness and shock and *fury* at what this place was trying to do to her.

The picture drew her gaze, but she forced focus away from the painting and kept walking down the hall. She would not fall into those traps. While ever she had the strength to stop it, she would fight. She would not let the house win. There was nothing this house could tell her that she hadn't been hearing for fifteen years, from others and from herself. What had it told the people before her? The ones locked into timeless torn images? Claire couldn't think about that now. Instead she reached down deep into her soul and focussed on two little girls playing joyfully, before any of this ever happened. She didn't stop her tread so that the house would know, but kept her pace.

It came as a surprise to see that up ahead the hall ended. Any sudden turns and twists were absent. What seemed to be ahead was a large arched window. Dim light was coming through; moonlight by the looks of it.

The thought made her pause; had she been in here that long already? Surely not. But then, maybe time worked differently here. The window was framed with intricate patterns that could still be made out despite being eroded by insects and filled with dust. It matched one of the external windows, the ones she had always thought of as the eyes of the skull.

Claire wasn't sure how any of this lined up, but she pushed away any inclination to try to make sense of this house as she approached the window. It would do no good, and only serve to confuse her.

Standing against the frame Claire found herself looking out over the front yard against a velvet night sky where silver light shone dimly through thick hanging clouds. She knew the village lay not far away, but at that time she could not see it for the cloud. She looked down into the front yard and her breath caught in her throat.

Two young girls were walking up towards the house. Claire's skin prickled with the danger. She raised a fist to bang on the glass, to yell and tell them to turn around but in the second it took her to do that she knew what she was looking at. Very slowly, she lowered her hand. It was almost funny, how terrified her younger self looked. At the time, she had fancied herself so very brave, but even from this distance she could make out the pale face and the barely concealed trembling. Sarah, right behind her, looked much the same.

She closed her eyes and rested her head against the glass. She wanted to run down and tell them to turn, wanted to smash this window and yell for them to run and never look back, but she knew that there would be no use.

"Go back," she whispered, despite herself.

She opened her eyes to see her younger self spin, looking around for the source of the voice. After a moment, eleven-year-old Claire convinced herself there was nothing and kept walking.

"Please," Claire said. To whom she didn't know.

The young Claire turned again.

And did not see what was just feet behind her. What in that moment made the older Claire's heart stop in her chest.

The figure wore a long, stained, ragged dress. Maybe it had been white once, but now it was mostly filth. Its face was skeletal; what skin remained was drawn tight over the bones, exposing rotten teeth in a horrible leer only slightly obscured by the stringy, dangling hair. It walked slowly, moving along at an almost leisurely pace, one foot after another.

The two girls could not see the figure, were not aware of its meandering pursuit. Had it been there, fifteen years ago? Had it been following her ever since?

The feeling began in the base of Claire's feet, a tingling prickling sensation that wound its way through every nerve causing shudders up over her shoulders up over her neck to the hairline at the base of her head. Claire turned.

And there the ragged she thing stood.

Claire didn't scream or run, despite the wave of panic that threatened to knock her over. She faced down the figure and felt her fists clench.

"Why?" she said. "Why us?"

The figure didn't reply. The grin stayed the same.

"We were kids," Claire said. "Just kids on a dare. Why did you have to punish us?"

Still, the figure neither moved nor spoke. Loathe to look away for the fear, Claire forced herself to look away. She returned her gaze to the two girls approaching the house.

They had reached the porch now, disappearing from her sight. She turned back to the skeletal woman. "If you want to hurt me, go ahead," Claire said, turning back to the woman who stood behind her. "I won't pretend I'm not scared. But you might as well know that I'm not leaving here without Sarah."

From the hall below, she heard the door open. Heard voices. If she walked back the way she had come, would she be face to face with herself? Was that what it was she couldn't remember?

The corpse seemed to read her thoughts, and somehow stood even more firmly in Claire's path.

Claire looked into those empty eye sockets, her voice threatened to die in her throat, but she forced it out.

"Where. Is. Sarah?"

There was no response. Below the footsteps of the two eleven-year-olds trod their way tentatively up the stairs. Claire could hear her own voice now, whispering to Sarah, trying to hide her fear as they drew closer.

And as she heard them reach the top of the stairs, from below came a terrible, piercing, agonised scream. As it did the skeletal figure vanished and Claire was alone, alone as she heard her younger self ask "What was that?" the terror now obvious.

"It was a scream," Sarah said. "Someone is in trouble!"

"We have to leave," younger Claire said. "We have to get out of here, this was a mistake Sarah, this was– "

"Someone is hurt!" The thudding footsteps, receded now, as the eleven-year-old girls went back down the stairs.

Claire ran to them rushing back down the hallway, past the picture frames, trying to reach the stairs and stop young Claire and Sarah before they ever reached what waited at the source of the scream. It was her chance, she could stop it now, before it started and turn it all around. Claire couldn't stop to think what might happen to her life right now, it only mattered that she reach them. Each stride forward, Claire thought should take her closer but the hall kept stretching ahead of her, longer and longer it seemed until she realised that she was running along a new hall towards a single door. She slowed, confused. She could no longer hear herself or Sarah. This door was not where she had come from.

A voice sounded in her head, intimately familiar, her own.

The only way out is through.

Claire strode forward and pushed open the door.

It was a bedroom; huge and old fashioned. The dresser was cluttered in cobwebbed hairbrushes and makeup utensils. The wardrobes were open and full of moth eaten clothes. But in the centre of the room stood a towering four poster bed. and lying on it...

It was the skeletal woman, but she wasn't alone. She clutched to her another body, dressed in the remains of a suit.

A suit stained with dark brown, long dried blood, all stemming from the knife driven into his chest.

Claire looked at them for several seconds, but there was no movement. These were just bodies. Nothing else. She bowed her head. "You killed them," she said. Terrible understanding had finally slid into place.

"You killed them and you let your hate and anger and guilt consume this house. And people knew. Everyone knew not to come here. But we were stupid enough to try, and when I left I took you with me. I let you out to do to our village what you did to this house. To slowly contaminate it until everybody started to feel what you felt."

She turned away. She couldn't look at the bodies anymore.

It was time to find Sarah and be gone from this place.

She walked back through the door and down the hall. In minutes, she arrived at the point where several corridors converged and found the one that led back to the stairs. Nothing shifted as she went. Nothing changed. She walked until she found the gap where the double doors had been, then, moving carefully, walked back on to the stairs.

Then she heard them.

"Sarah, I think they were right. I think this place really is haunted."

"That was a scream Claire. Someone through here needs help."

"But if—"

"What if it's not a haunted house? What if someone else came here and is in trouble?"

Claire moved quickly and quietly down the stairs towards the voices. Once at the bottom she stepped around to the door opposite the one she had gone through before. Her younger self and Sarah stood there, still arguing. Claire looked on, her heart wretched with longing to avert the next moments that would surely come.

"Let's just go home," young Claire pleaded. "Let's go home and forget we ever came here."

"Do it," present day Claire said. "Turn around and walk away."

Young Claire glanced over her shoulder, eyes wide as she looked for the source of the voice. She looked straight through her older self.

"Run," Claire said. "Listen to me, you have to run."

"Sarah…" the younger Claire said, eyes still searching. "I think… I think we should go. Something…"

"We have to at least check." Sarah reached for the door handle.

"Don't!" Older and younger Claire screamed at the same time as Sarah opened the door. Through it was only blackness and then, with a sound like the last moment of water draining out of a sink, Sarah was gone. The door slammed shut. Eleven-year old Claire, screaming, grabbed it and tried to open it, but it wouldn't budge.

She slammed her fist against it, again and again, calling Sarah's name, calling until her throat was hoarse and her breathing was ragged and she fell to her knees, begging Sarah to return.

Claire stood there and watched and remembered, remembered how it had felt; the terror, the desperation, the slowly growing hopelessness. The hours waiting here for a friend who would never return, until finally she decided to turn around and get help only to step into the sunlight and find she could not remember what had happened to her, only that it had been something terrible and now Sarah was gone.

And as she remembered, her still weeping younger self faded before her eyes, like dust blown away on the wind.

And once again it was just her and the house; Claire Anderson, twenty-six years old, standing alone and staring at the door through which her friend had vanished, and at the door she could not open.

She knew, somehow, that that would not be the case now. She knew as clearly as she knew that if she turned and walked through the front door of the house it would open for her and she could leave this place, again with no memory of what had happened inside. She could leave and nobody would be any the wiser. Nobody else had been lost this time. She could vanish and put it all behind her, knowing that the house could not be bested. Or she could walk through that door, face whatever was on the other side, and know that she would probably never come out.

She walked over and opened the door.

Chapter Eight - Beyond the Door

Something had changed. No. Not something. *Everything*.

She felt different. Before walking through the door, she had been tired, in pain from bruises and scratches, out of breath from her run upstairs. Now she felt... fresh. New. And yet somehow less. She had more energy but it would expend quicker. Her strength wasn't the same and yet... yet why did this feel so familiar? It was strange and yet she was sure she knew exactly how this felt because she had been like this before.

Then she looked down at her hands. Small. Much smaller than her own. Her arms were skinny and her body was entirely different. But she recognised it because it *was* her own. Or at least it had been fifteen years ago.

She looked around the room. In contrast to the rest of the house, this was different. Well lit, although where the light was coming from she couldn't be sure. It was adorned with huge, colourful paintings, and the floor was scattered with toys. At the far end was a dollhouse, an exact replica of this house, similar to the one she had found earlier but this was resplendent, in its prime, not decrepit nor dripping with blood.

And crouching in front of it...

"Hello Claire." Sarah turned to her with a smile.

"Sarah," Claire said.

"I thought you would have been right behind me," Sarah said, as casually as if they were discussing the weather. "But you took so long."

"Fifteen years," Claire said.

"Wow," Sarah said. "That's a very long time."

"Yes, it is," Claire said. "Have you been here the whole time?"

Sarah nodded. "It didn't feel so long to me. Or maybe it did. It's hard to tell here." She picked up a little doll, opened the house and placed it in one of the rooms before looking around for another.

"You're still so young," Claire said.

"So are you," Sarah replied. "You haven't aged a day."

"I guess not," Claire replied, remembering how she looked at that moment. "What happened, Sarah? You went through the door, you disappeared and... and then what?"

Sarah paused midway to picking up another toy. She frowned. It was the look of somebody remembering something they would prefer not to.

"I was lost," she said. "For a while. I was in a bad place. And then she found me."

"Who?" Claire said, despite knowing the answer.

"Mother." Sarah's face split into a wide grin. "She took me in, gave me this room. And she has taken care of me ever since. She stopped all the people who tried to take me away from her. She kept me safe. She let me see what was going on.

Some of it, anyway. And whatever she could, she gave me. It has been just *wonderful*." Claire shivered at that.

She looked away, trying to think. "You know who she is, you know what she did — right?"

"Who is that?" Sarah's voice was light and airy, but there was an unmistakeable edge to it. "What did she do?"

"She murdered her children," Claire said.

"I *am* her child."

"No." Claire could hear desperation in her voice now. "No, you're not Sarah. You have parents, parents who loved you and mourned you."

Sarah looked at her without expression.

"Sarah, whoever this… this woman was, it's her fault this happened. She trapped you here. She killed everyone who came to save you. And she poisoned our village."

"No, she didn't," Sarah said.

"Yes, she did!" Claire cried. "You haven't seen it Sarah. It's falling apart at the seams. The plants don't grow, the businesses are all dying, the whole place is in disrepair and nobody can bring themselves to either fix it or to just… *leave*. When we came here we let her out and she's been destroying our home ever since."

"No, she hasn't," Sarah said.

"She has!" Claire's frustration was spilling over now. "You haven't *seen it.*"

"Yes, I have," Sarah said, still so calm. "I've seen all of it. I'm the one who did it."

For a moment silence hung over the room.

Claire stared at Sarah, mouth hanging open, trying to make sense of what she had just heard. And then, slowly, her eyes moved to one of the pictures on the wall, hanging right over the dollhouse

It was a framed map. Except it had been scribbled all over in jagged, angry spikes of black pencil.

"It was you," Claire said.

"Mother doesn't care about the village," Sarah said. 'They never did anything to her."

"What did they do to you?" Claire demanded.

"Nothing," Sarah said. "It's not about what they did to me. It's about what they did to *you.*"

Claire looked again at the serene, smiling young girl who had once been her best friend; so gentle and kind, sacrificing herself all because she heard a scream and was sure someone needed help.

Sarah - so loved, the best friend anyone could ever ask for, who had spent years destroying the village that demonised her best friend.

"You shouldn't have done that," Claire said.

"You'd have done the same for me," Sarah said, turning back to the dollhouse. "I saw it, Claire. All of it. I saw my parents screaming at you when your family went for dinner at the pub. I saw them yelling until the manager had to ask you to leave. I saw you sitting by yourself at school. I saw them trip you in the halls and steal your lunch. I saw them burn your books and laugh at you and call you murderer. I saw people looking away whenever they saw you in the street.

I saw the teacher who tried to have you expelled for failing a maths test. I saw all of their hate and spite and anger and I couldn't take it.

Not when you did nothing wrong. They hurt you for no reason. So I hurt them."

A wave of empathy passed through Claire. "They hurt me because they didn't know any better. They hurt me because *they* were hurting. It wasn't their fault."

"Wasn't it?" Sarah was not looking at her; focusing on arranging the dolls in the house. "They were the adults. They were the ones who were supposed to guide us and show us the right path. Kids are allowed to not know any better. Adults have to."

"But they *don't*,' Claire said. 'They make mistakes, Sarah. They mess up too. Nothing really changes except you have responsibilities."

"You thought you had a responsibility to come here?"

"Of course I did," Claire said. "I want to bring you home."

"But she is home," a voice from behind them said.

CAT KNIGHT

Chapter Nine - The Power of Mother

She was no longer skeletal. Not in this room. She was smiling and beautiful, her hair thick and long, her face full, her dress pure white. She stood in the doorway and beamed at Sarah as Claire backed away.

"She's happy here," the woman said. "Aren't you Sarah?"

"I am, Mother," Sarah said.

"She doesn't know any better," Claire said. "You've kept her captive for years."

"I gave her a home," the woman said. "I took care of her. That is what a mother does."

"You're right," Claire said. "A mother takes care of her children. She doesn't kill them then try to find a substitute."

The woman froze. Her smile seemed to falter. For the first time she looked at Claire and for just a moment her face was that horrible, wasted skeleton again. But in seconds her full features and sweet smile were back.

"And what would you know, Claire Anderson?" the woman said. "All those lovers who came and went.

All those late nights, drinking alone. All the nightmares at the hate and..." her eyes flickered to Claire's wrist. "And the other things."

"I know because I lived through it all and faced it," Claire said. "I'm still facing it.

I do every day. Because I never once tried to pretend it didn't happen, or replace it with some twisted fantasy."

The woman seemed rooted to the spot. Claire took a step forward.

"You killed them," Claire said. "You needed help and nobody gave it to you. Nobody knew how."

"Enough," the woman whispered.

"The only way out is through," Claire said. "You want to know how I did it?" She looked back at Sarah. "After years, I forgave myself. And I knew that meant I had to come here and end it. To do that I had to forgive the village as well. I had to forgive them for how they treated me and then I needed do the right thing. To come back for Sarah."

She looked back at the woman.

"You can't hurt me," Claire said. "Because I don't hate you. I *understand* you. And since you can't do it yourself, since no-one left alive will ever do it for you, I'm going to. I forgive you."

The woman's eyes had gone wide. Her mouth gaped.

Claire turned fully back to Sarah.

"You need to forgive them," Claire said. "All of them. Because it wasn't your punishment to give."

"They hurt you," Sarah said.

"They're not the first and they won't be the last." Claire knelt in front of her friend. She took Sarah's face in her hands and smiled through the tears she could not stop. "I'm sorry Sarah. For all of it. I never should have made you come here. I didn't know any better, but even so. Can you forgive me?"

Sarah held Claire's gaze for a long time.

"No Sarah," the woman said from behind them. "No. She's trying to take you away. She's trying to steal you from me."

Sarah's eyes flickered over Claire's shoulder to Mother and then back to Claire's face.

"Sarah," Claire said. "Enough is enough. Enough people have suffered. Please. Let it end."

Sarah closed her eyes.

"Sarah!" the woman screamed.

Claire ignored her. She pulled Sarah into an embrace and locked her with a gaze, no longer fearing the woman or the house. Because Claire had figured it out.

The woman's power came from hate and fear; yet, it was not her own, but the power came from the hate and fear which others felt for her. The woman had simply turned it against them, driving them mad, imprisoning them and burning them away with illusions. But Claire wasn't scared of her because Claire saw her for what she was and she pitied her.

"Sarah, the only way out is through." Sarah nodded.

And like that, everything changed.

Chapter Ten - The Return of Sarah

It took Sarah a moment to recognise where she was. And another to realise that she was looking at daylight.

The hill where the house had stood was bare, but for the few shards of a broken foundation. Beyond that there was nothing but the tangle of bushes and long dead trees. Above her the clouds had broken open, the golden sun pouring down over it all. In that glow, even the dead vegetation didn't seem so bad.

Sarah frowned. She could not quite remember how she had gotten here. She remembered walking into the house – had a house been here? – but that felt so long ago. And then was someone she had called mother but...

Mother. Mum. Her parents.

Then she remembered them, so clearly. The last time she had seen them was before she and... what was her friend's name? Well whoever it was, before they had headed out to do something that had seemed important at the time. Now it seemed vague and distant.

Her parents must be worried sick. She wasn't sure how long she had been here, but she was going to be in so much trouble when she arrived back home. Well, no point in holding it off. She took a deep breath and started to walk back towards the distant village.

Over the next few days the village was abuzz with whispers and rumours. There was so much that nobody could explain – true, that had been the case for a long time in this place – but now the circumstances were stranger than ever.

How did you explain an eleven-year old girl who had gone missing fifteen years ago suddenly arriving on her parents' doorstep, with no clear memory of where she had been and no visible signs of aging? And beyond that, there was the old house on the hill, which had vanished, leaving behind only ruins that looked like they had been crumbling for over a hundred years. And then there were the flowers; granted it was only a handful, but nobody could remember seeing a flower growing here in years.

But perhaps the strangest thing was something more intangible. An overpowering sense that *something* had lifted, pervaded the village.

The sun shone a little brighter, village folk regained the energy and passion they'd been missing for so long. Day by day the streets filled up again, people slowly setting out and doing their business in broad daylight for the first time in a very, very long time greeting each other with warmth and goodwill. It was like the dawn of summer after a very long winter.

Here and there, however, there were hints of sadness.

Old Mr and Mrs Anderson still kept to themselves, and when people *did* see them their eyes seemed to be focused on the hill where the house had once stood, the expressions on their face hopeful. One child had come back, so maybe another could as well.

And then there was Kev, whose business boomed in a way it hadn't for years, and yet he seemed somehow diminished, often lost in thought even as the kids started coming back in.

Sometimes the door would open and he would look up, then swiftly sink back into whatever thoughts held him when the person he hoped for didn't walk through.

On the day Sarah had come back the whole village were so focused on this strange miracle, so bewildered by what had happened, that none of them noticed the lone woman making her way to the train station, sitting on the platform in the sun with a slight smile until the train arrived and she stepped on it. She wasn't going back to London. She didn't know where she was going. One day soon, when the relief had faded into joy and she was certain she was truly free, she would let her parents know she was safe and well. Perhaps she would even visit, but for now, all she knew was that the only way out was through. And now she was out.

The End

Thank-You for Reading

The Haunting of Knoll House.

I hope you enjoyed it and would very much appreciate

it if you could take a few minutes to

Leave A Review

Over the page you'll find a preview of

The Haunting of Stone Street Cemetery

Here is Your Preview of The Haunting of Stone Street Cemetery

Chapter One - The Cemetery

"How many more of these do we have?" Lauren asked.

Lauren, with her red hair, made an unlikely vampire, but she did make a pretty one. At thirty, Lauren had added a few more curves to her high school figure, as people who worked at a desk were apt to do.

"I don't know," Charlotte answered. "Two weeks till Halloween. Two more parties?" Charlotte, "Charlie", was also thirty. Short, dark hair, striped shirt, whistle, she looked like the referee she pretended to be. That she taught physical education at a local school enhanced her Halloween image.

"At least two," Monica said. She was the third member of this threesome that had been together almost since nappies. She was also the prettiest. Long blonde hair, blue eyes, a figure that looked absolutely wonderful in her short, black mini dress and apron with white lace trim, her thigh high stockings, and saucy headpiece, she was every man's fantasy of a naughty French maid. "Maybe three," she added.

"Three? I think I'm going to puke." Lauren weaved to one side.

"Don't fight it," Charlie said. "Better to get it out than to let it bubble up your throat."

"Oh, great," Lauren said. "That's wonderful advice."

A cloud crossed the moon, and the street turned noticeably darker. Monica blinked, checking to see if it was her eyes. To one side, Charlie grabbed Lauren's arm, steading her. They were coming home late because it had been a good costume party.

Plenty of alcohol and snacks and people who thought they were clever, and some of them were. Monica had been particularly captivated by a superhero in tights who had painted a big 'S' on his bare chest. At some point during the party, she discovered that the 'S' was edible—at least a woman in a nurse costume thought so. Well, maybe the nurse just wanted to lick Superman's skin. That seemed OK too.

"Is it getting colder, or is it me?' Monica asked.

"If you wore a skirt that covered your arse, you might be a bit warmer," Charlie said.

"French Maids don't wear long skirts," Monica answered.

"I need to get home," Lauren said. "I'm going to be sick."

"We're on our way," Charlie said. "We're on our way."

Ahead, a single, faint streetlight cast a small circle of light. Despite being intoxicated, Monica could see why the streets were dangerous at night. There was no way to know if something evil lurked in the shadows. A single woman would make a likely victim.

For a moment, she wondered how that thought slipped into her mind.

She was with two friends, and there was no danger within a hundred miles. She shook her head to clear the thought as it started to drizzle.

"Oh, great," Lauren said. "Cold and wet."

"It's just a mist," Charlie said. "We'll be home and warm before you know it."

"Who had the best costume?" Monica asked, trying to change the subject.

"That's easy," Charlie said. "The princess."

"The princess?" Lauren said. "Wasn't she a crossdresser? I thought she was a he."

"Not a chance," Charlie said. "I talked to her. She's definitely female."

"I don't know how you can tell," Monica said. "Anymore, the he's look like she's and the she's look like he's."

"Anyway," Lauren said and burped. "I thought the guy dressed like Dracula looked the best. I thought his fangs were real."

"That's because you're a vampire," Charlie said. "Bats stick together."

Lauren laughed briefly. "Oh god, don't make me laugh. My head is spinning."

"I thought Superman was right up there," Monica said. "Pecs and abs, ladies, pecs and abs."

"Oh, I'm sick," Lauren said. "Get me home."

The rain fell harder, more than a drizzle but not yet a downpour. Monica knew her pigtails would soon look like drowned rats sticking out from her head. And her tight blouse would be more fitting for a wet T-shirt contest than a costume party. If she hadn't been mostly drunk, she would have been upset — that and the fact that she didn't have to work the next day.

"Well," Monica began. "If you want to get home as fast as possible, we can take our old route."

"Through the cemetery?" Lauren asked. "That one?"

"That one," Monica answered.

"It's dark," Charlie said. "We never went that way in the dark."

"It's a cemetery," Monica said. "Dead bodies buried under six feet of dirt. I don't think we have to worry."

"I don't know... Kahil warned me to be careful what I did around Halloween. She said everything ramps up."

"Charlie. COME ON. You don't really believe that!"

"I've got an open mind. Just because you don't believe in ghosts."

"I know about your psychic," Monica said to Charlie, "and I'm guessing she talks to the spirits all the time. But, frankly, I don't buy it. I mean, I've done some research."

"You didn't do any research, your assistant did," Charlie said.

"Well OK, but I read what she found. And trust me, she didn't find any evidence of the afterlife."

"You're like all the others, mind closed to what are infinite possibilities."

"Stop arguing," Lauren said. "Get me home. God, how many streetlights are there?"

"One," Charlie answered. "Why?"

"I hate double vision."

Monica reached out and grabbed Lauren's arm. "Come on, we'll cut through the cemetery, and we'll be home thirty minutes earlier."

"I don't think that's a good idea," Charlie said.

"Nonsense," Monica said. "It's raining and cold, and Lauren is about to pass out.

Want to carry her home? Charlie glanced at Monica but said nothing as Monica turned into an alley.

Lauren leaned heavily on Monica's arm, barely keeping her balance. While the street had been dark, it was like a neon-lit arcade compared to the alley. Monica was half thankful for the cold rain as it probably kept the rats at bay. Not that she was particularly scared of rats—as long as they maintained a proper distance. The alley was theirs. She was willing to grant them ownership. If they didn't run over her toes, she was happy.

"What's that smell?" Lauren asked. "It's making me sick."

"Rubbish," Charlie answered. "Breathe through your mouth."

"We'll be through this soon," Monica added. "Hang on."

They moved quickly through the alley. Her TV station had run a program about muggings, and she knew alleys housed almost as many muggers as rats. They walked along another street with a distant streetlight, Lauren moaning and Charlie silent.

Monica asked herself why she hadn't left with Superman when he had asked. She would be home by now. But she wouldn't be with her friends. They had developed a kind of pact. No one could leave with someone new. Phone numbers were fine. Arranging a date was fine. But if the women arrived together, they left together. Monica was thankful for that. Just before they left the alley, they stopped as a wet, black cat scampered past.

"Was that a rat?" Lauren asked.

"A cat," Charlie said. "A black cat."

"Come on," Monica said.

"It's bad luck, isn't it?" Lauren asked.

"We're not going to worry about bad luck," Monica said. "The rain is unlucky enough."

The arch over the path announced their destination — STONE STREET CEMETERY.

A yellow light shone on the name, reminding Monica of her school days. The three of them had often giggled their way through this entrance. Sometimes, they ran, and if they did, Charlie always won. More often, they walked, chatting about school and boys and teachers and homework. Rain, sun, fog, they used the path often.

But never at night.

Charlie had been right about that. They had never walked through the rows of headstones and graves in the dark. Monica wasn't sure if that was because they had been scared or because they hadn't really had the opportunity. In those days, perhaps Charlie had purposely steered them around the cemetery. If she did, Monica never noticed. Avoiding a dark cemetery seemed like a bright idea.

"Why is it so effing dark?" Lauren asked.

"It's night," Charlie answered.

Lauren fumbled through her purse until she found her phone. Blinking, she tapped the screen until the torch app came up. Suddenly, a beam of light shone ahead of her.

"That's better," Lauren said.

"Your battery is going to die in like a minute," Charlie said.

"I don't care," Lauren said. "I hate to walk in the dark." They were halfway through the cemetery when Monica felt the urge. "Oh god," she said suddenly stopping and crossing her legs. "I have to stop."

"What?" Charlie asked. "We can't stop, not here."

Monica danced around in circles. "I can't wait." She stepped off the path into the dark.

"I'm going to puke," Lauren said.

"I can't believe the both of you. You can't be doing this," Charlie said. "This is a graveyard!"

"It's not like I'm not going to wee on a grave," Monica said from out of the dark.

She moved around a headstone and onto some grass. The problem was that in the rainy dark, it was impossible to know exactly where she was. She hoped it wasn't a grave, and she hoped she could hurry up and finish what she was doing before someone else came along. All she needed was some Bobby or caretaker coming by. How long would she have her job if that story got into the tabloids? Not long. She tried to hurry, but she was not a practiced camper.

"Hurry," Lauren said. "My phone is dying."

"Smile," Charlie said.

Monica looked up, and Charlie's phone flashed.

"You took my picture?"

"Hurry up, or I'll sell it to the Guardian."

"You wouldn't dare. Of course I wouldn't Ms Stanford."

"At least, not tonight. I'll save it for when I need a favour."

Monica heard Charlie move off giggling.

"Want to see a picture of our esteemed telly friend?" Charlie said. "That's Monica," Lauren said. "But why is she squatting on someone's grave?"

"Oh god," Charlie said yelled. "Monica, get out of there!"

Monica came sheepishly around the headstone to find Charlie and Lauren looking at Charlie's phone.

"Show me," Monica said.

Charlie showed Monica the photo, and the headstone behind Monica was clearly visible.

"Delete it," Monica said. "Delete it now."

"I will, I will," Charlie said.

"OUCH!" Lauren's voice sounded from the dark.

Charlie and Monica turned to Lauren who had stepped off the path and tripped over a low grave marker. They hurried over and helped Lauren to her feet.

"Let's get out of here," Charlie said. "This is getting eerie."

Charlie took Lauren's left arm, and Monica took Lauren's right. Even though Monica didn't feel scared, she agreed with Charlie. It was time to leave the cemetery. Weird things begat weird things. Or, as they said at the station—bad luck comes in threes.

It was raining harder as they exited the cemetery. Monica was soaked and cold as a brisk wind arose. Why hadn't they called a cab? They would be safe and warm and not worried about bad juju or karma or whatever people called retribution for weeing on a grave. Luckily, Lauren's house was only a block away. Actually, it was her parents' house. Lauren had bought it from them so they could retire to the north. Lauren lived alone which was fine since it was a small house.

"I'm going to be sick," Lauren said as they reached the house.

Lauren closed one eye and tried to smile. "Thanks, mates, I don't think I could have done it without you." Then, she started giggling. "You two look so funny. I want a pic."

Monica and Charlie watched Lauren fumble with her purse... and fumble with her purse.

"It's not here," Lauren said.

"What's not there?" Monica asked.

"My phone. It's not here. I lost it."

"Check your pockets," Charlie said. "You probably misplaced it."

Monica watched as Lauren checked the few pockets in her vampire costume. "It's not here," Lauren said.

"Then, you lost it," Charlie said.

"We have to go find it," Lauren said.

"You're in no condition to look for anything tonight. Tomorrow is soon enough," Monica said.

"You don't understand," Lauren said. "My client list is on that phone. I can't lose it."

"We don't have any idea where you lost it," Charlie said. "And it's raining. Go to bed."

"The cemetery, I lost it in the cemetery. Remember, I was using the torch, and then, and then…"

"We're not going back to the cemetery in the dark," Monica said. "But I promise we'll be back in the morning. Then, we'll all go find your phone. All right?"

Lauren began to cry. "I need my phone."

"Not tonight, Lauren. You're not making any deals tonight." Charlie gently turned Lauren and helped her up the steps and in through the front door. "Go in and sleep. We'll be back in the morning."

Monica waited on the walk as Charlie coaxed Lauren into the house. Since she couldn't get any wetter, Monica didn't mind too much. "I'm guessing she won't remember losing her phone," Charlie said as she re-joined Monica.

"She never does," Monica said. "Next time, we dump her in a cab."

"Along with you and me."

They laughed as they trudged through the rain. Luckily. Charlie's flat wasn't far, and the rain didn't get worse. The two-floor climb to the flat tired Monica more than she wanted to admit. She felt the effects of the alcohol.

"When will your new house be ready?" Charlie asked as she tossed a towel to Monica.

"Monday, and I can't thank you enough for the last week." Monica undid her pigtails and vigorously dried her hair.

"You're welcome, and I'm sure you'll find a way of paying me back. Good night."

Monica watched Charlie disappear into the bedroom before she went to the loo and stripped off her wet clothes. She draped them over the tub to dry and slipped into her PJ's. As she brushed her teeth, she wondered if she had really done a wee on someone's grave. That thought made her shudder. That was really bad luck, wasn't it? Like walking under a ladder or opening an umbrella indoors? Although, she would have paid a pretty penny for an umbrella before she left the party.

After making her bed on the sofa, Monica turned out the light and closed her eyes. Then, she opened them as a cloud moved, and the moon shone through the window.

For a moment, Monica swore she saw a figure looking into the room, a face but not really a face. She blinked and the face was gone. She shivered as she watched the window for a full minute. The face didn't appear, and she presumed she had imagined the entire episode. That was the last thing she remembered before Charlie shook her awake.

"Come on," Charlie said. "Get dressed. Lauren's not answering her home phone."

Chapter Two - The Consequence

Monica was up and dressed in a flash. While they had walked the night before, this being Sunday, they drove Monica's car to Lauren's house. When they found the front door unlocked, Monica frowned at Charlie.

"Lauren usually locks it, doesn't she?"

Charlie nodded and pushed open the door.

"Should we go in?" Monica asked. "I mean, if something happened, shouldn't we call the police?"

"The door's unlocked. She's our friend. We don't have time for Bobbies."

The house was exactly as Monica remembered, nothing was out of place, but she was still surprised to find the lights on.

"She's probably passed out," Charlie said as she led the way to the bedroom.

But Lauren was not passed out. In fact, she wasn't in the bedroom. More importantly, her bed had not been slept in.

"Check the house," Monica said. "Let's see if we can find her."

It took less than five minutes for Charlie and Monica to look into every room and closet. When they met back by the front door, they frowned at one another.

"She's not here," Charlie said.

"She wasn't here all night. You don't suppose..."

"As drunk as she was, she wasn't going out to meet some chap."

"Where are her clothes?" Monica asked.

"Her what?"

"Her wet clothes. She was as soaked as we were. Her wet vampire costume should be here somewhere."

"I didn't see it."

"Neither did I."

They nodded at the same time.

"Her phone," Charlie said.

"The cemetery," Monica said.

They hurried along the street, not bothering with the car, but cutting across the backstreets and passing through the alley way.

"That dumb skirt," Charlie said as they entered the back gate into the cemetery "In the dark and rain, what could she hope to find?"

"Her client list. Like she couldn't find more clients. I swear, when I find that girl I'm going to give a good chat. She can't be doing things like this."

They hurried along the still wet and slippery path.

"It's just ahead, isn't it?" Charlie asked.

"What's just ahead?" Monica answered.

"Where we stopped, where you had a wee on a grave."

"Don't, Charlie, don't say that out loud. It's bad enough that I did it...without knowing it. I don't need anyone reminding me."

They turned a corner and spotted Lauren. Charlie stopped dead for a split second then sprinted forward. When she reached her, her voice wailed out, "Oh God. No. It can't be" A weight dropped in Monica's stomach.

"I'll call emergency", she called in an unnaturally high-pitched voice. Monica punched the key pad. She didn't have to say much. The dispatcher assured Monica that help was on the way. Had Monica been with Charlie and Lauren, she would have told the dispatcher that the help needn't hurry. As soon as Monica saw Lauren's blue face she knew that the worst had happened.

On one knee, Charlie looked up, tears in her eyes. Monica knelt and wrapped an arm around Charlie. Monica didn't say anything. There was nothing to say. They cried together until the police arrived.

For the police, it was easy. Lauren tripped, hit her head, and became unconscious. Then she aspirated; she choked on her own vomit. Just another young woman who had behaved recklessly and had too much to drink. Case closed. For Monica, it wasn't that simple. It was a guilt trip because she could have stayed the night with Lauren. If Monica had, Lauren would be alive.

Monica told herself over and over that it wasn't her fault. Over and over, she felt a twinge of pain. Even Lauren's parents had told Monica and Charlie through their tears that Lauren's death was not their fault, it was a tragic wasted life brought on by bad judgement. And they should be grateful they were still here, and to live their lives to the fullest making every moment count. As if that erased the guilt. It was after the funeral, while they sipped punch at Lauren's house, that Charlie took Monica aside.

"You think it was an accident?" Charlie asked. Monica rubbed her temples, she didn't feel like listening to Charlies juju superstition.

"Of course, what else could it be?"

"Remember what you did?"

"Yeah, I got drunk. So did you."

"No, on the way home, remember the cemetery?"

"Of course, I remember the cemetery I had to have a wee so what?"

"You did it on a grave. On a person's grave. Have any idea what that might do? Especially at bloody Halloween."

"Nothing, absolutely nothing. Blokes take a leak all over graves and headstones all the time. Do they die?"

"You're not listening. Kahil says that sometimes spirits take offense when someone disrespects their grave. And they get back at them."

"Is this Kahil, the psychic?"

"Kahil is very knowledgeable about spiritual things."

"Kahil is a sinkhole for quid. What do you expect her to say? That spirits love when a chap waters the grave?"

"I'm just saying that if you did something on the wrong grave, the spirit might have taken it out on Lauren."

"Don't be daft. Lauren died because she made an incredibly bad decision, which isn't hard to believe since she was DEAD DRUNK. She paid for her stupidity."

Charlie took a step back. "You didn't like Lauren?"

Monica rubbed her face. "I loved Lauren. We both did. But I'm not about to accept responsibility for her death."

Charlie backed away.

"Wait," Monica said.

"What happens next is on your head," Charlie said.

"Oh, come on Charlie you don't mean that, let's talk."

Charlie shook her head, turned, and walked away. Monica let her go. She knew better than to test Charlie's belief in the supernatural. Charlie had been partial to ghosts and spirits and paranormal phenomena since school.

"You're coming to the house warming," Monica called.

Charlie didn't answer.

The Haunting of Stone Street Cemetery

Available at

http://a-fwd.to/1txL6vk

Here is Your Preview of The Haunting of Highcliff Hall

Prologue

Highcliff Hall

Tràchd Romhra

Anglo-Scottish Border

1702

Mallory was a great beauty. Her hair was fair, nigh to a silvery moon, her eyes sparkled blue as the ocean, encircled with a light green ring. It was not a surprise that the Laird Spruce would seek to take the nubile blonde-haired beauty who held the promise of lips as sweet as cherries. His loins stirred when he heard the talk of her from the lewd tongues of his men. Now, someone had betrayed her, perhaps in exchange for keeping their tongue from being severed from its filthy mouth.

Unannounced he rode through the village, until he found her and brought her to his keep. Mallory's weeping could be heard for days and nights throughout the Hall.

He roared with laughter when they brought her betrothed to him. Young and strong, but no match for the men of the keep, they caught him on his mission to free young Mallory. But Instead of fleeing with her to safety, he now stood manacled to the wall of Spruce's dungeon.

Spruce tortured him with descriptions of the lustful deflowering, holding the blood-stained garments to his face. Fury contorted young MacDougal's body as he tore at the chains that bound him. Unable to free himself he spat at the Laird. It caught him fair in the left eye. Spruce beat MacDougal till he almost died.

That night, the Laird Spruce relayed the sordid tale to Mallory. If she treated Spruce well, Spruce would let MacDougal live, but if she did not perform her duties willingly, MacDougal would rot in the manacles that bound him. Mallory paled, whiter than her hair, for she knew, in the end, the Laird would torture Ian MacDougal to death.

The next day with her head covered, disguised as a crone, she slipped from the castle after knocking out the servant girl he brought to tend her needs. Once clear of the gate, Mallory ran, her heart beating like thunder in her chest. There would be no escape, save one. When she reached the cliff-edge she didn't stop.

When Laird Spruce learned of the loss of his fair young conquest, rage took him. Calling on his henchman, Spruce sped to the dungeon. MacDougal was beaten to his last breath, and with it he brought the curse of hell down on the Laird. Whomever was born from his loins would not survive it, but the shadow of death would follow them until the last Spruce was wiped from the earth. And even to the men that protected this spawn of evil, all would be cast to the pit of hell along with their Laird for eternity. MacDougal's body was left to rot chained to the dungeon walls.

But with the coming of the new moon, the Laird's henchman fell ill from madness and threw himself over the cliff.

They found him mangled and broken, empty sockets seeing nothing. Spruce's men began to fear for MacDougal's mother had been a healer, a hag.

What powers of the hex did MacDougal possess? A terror besieged them. A plan was formed with pike, axe, and sword, they pummelled Spruce to the cliff edge. Justice would be done for Mallory Breac and Ian MacDougal.

CAT KNIGHT

Chapter One - The Hag's Prophecy

Highcliff Hall

The Solway Firth

Anglo-Scottish Border

September 2017

"I'm going to miss this place." Catherine Davidson looked across the pub to the bar and its cohort of grinning men. The Dancing Hawk had been her watering hole of choice since she was twenty. Cosy, familiar, it was a copy of a thousand other pubs in London, each with their dart boards and raucous talk.

"Then, don't go," Sheila said. "Why would you want to live in that godforsaken neck of the woods in the first place?"

"You know why. I'm tired of the road. I've been around the world for Auntie Beeb, and what have I got to show for it?"

"Well, there are those trophies, right there." Sheila glanced at the white, round marks on Catherine's wrists born from spending several days in handcuffs, captured by mercenaries in Afghanistan. 'Trophies'.

Battle scars born in the line of duty for a foreign correspondent. Catherine took a deep breath and let it out a sigh of relief that never left her, when she recalled the memory. "Don't remind me. That's was undoubtedly the most dangerous thing I've ever done. If my interpreter hadn't known the cousin of a cousin of a cousin, I'd be in some harem in the middle of the desert."

"But Highcliff Hall? That doesn't even sound hospitable."

Catherine smiled at Sheila who had been her best friend for ten years, even before they both went to work for the Beeb. Catherine liked to think she had aged better than Sheila who had piled on the pounds of motherhood. Catherine supposed that the satisfaction of two children made the weight worthwhile, but she wasn't convinced. While she had met a couple of men she might share her bed with, they had never quite qualified for marriage. If they had asked… She avoided that "what if…".

"I'm assured Highcliff Hall is perfectly liveable. It has grounds, a caretaker, and a housekeeper. I won't even have to dust or cook. And, it comes with a small stipend for upkeep."

"Yes, but what will you do? Oh, I know, that great novel you've been outlining since puberty. 'Romance Under the Stars.' Was that it?"

"All heathens mock what they do not understand."

"Did you steal that title? I distinctly remember hearing it before."

"Google it and find out."

"I'm not that desperate, although I did Google your Highcliff Hall. Do you have any idea how old it is?"

"Yeah, centuries. It's been in that branch of the family since before Adam left Eden, or so it seems. And it would still be in that branch if grand aunt what's-her-name hadn't died. She was my grandmother's sister and the last of them, may she rest in peace."

Catherine looked across the room and spotted an old, bent woman in a black shawl sliding between the tables with a familiarity Catherine didn't quite understand.

"Who is that?"

"Who?"

"That old woman. What is she doing?"

"The Hag? She's trying to get drunk."

"Begging?"

"The Hag doesn't beg. She reads your future for a pint. And I have to admit, sometimes, she's quite funny."

"You bought her a pint?"

"Of course, and she told me I was pregnant long before the test did. Then again, most people look at me and guess I'm pregnant. It's my shape I think. And don't try to spare my feelings. I have no illusions as to my figure and nothing but envy for yours."

"You know correspondents never eat while they're working."

"So, that's the secret. One more thing, the Hag—"

"Does she have a real name?"

"I've never heard anyone use it. Anyway, the Hag also told me it would be a boy, but that's not so magical since that's a fifty-fifty chance."

At that moment, the old woman shuffled to Catherine's table. Up close, the woman was uglier and more misshapen than Catherine had imagined. She smelled too. Catherine guessed Thai or Indian spices, but she couldn't be sure.

"Your future for a pint," the Hag rasped.

Sheila waved to a waitress who nodded and headed for the bar. "Not me," Sheila told the Hag. "Read her future."

For some reason, Catherine had no desire to hear the Hag say a word. Catherine had attended all sorts of magical ceremonies in all manner of countries, and she had never felt one iota of fear. Whether the shaman or witch doctor had worn face paint or a bone through his nose made no difference.

For Catherine, it was all phony, jazzed up chants and dances for the gullible. Yet, this smelly woman, this Hag made Catherine's skin crawl. It was as if she expected the Hag to bring forth an evil eye.

"You don't believe," the Hag told Catherine. "That's my curse. I tell nothing but the truth, and no one believes. No matter. I'm a cheap show. A pint for what you will never believe. I'm like those fakirs you took photos of."

"You? You know my work?" Catherine asked.

"I know your days of chasing stories are over."

"Everyone knows that. I signed off last night."

"Yes, yes, you did."

The waitress arrived with a pint of ale and set it on the table. The Hag eyed the drink as if it was ambrosia, the nectar of the gods. But she didn't reach for it as Catherine expected. Instead, the Hag looked Catherine in the eye and grabbed her hand.

The strong grip surprised Catherine, and she fought the urge to jerk back. Instead, she forced a smile.

The Hag laughed. "You control your emotions well." Then, she studied Catherine's paw.

As Catherine waited, the old woman shuddered. She let go of Catherine and started to turn away.

"Wait," Sheila said. "Your pint."

"Keep it," the Hag said.

"You owe Catherine a telling."

"No, she doesn't," Catherine said.

"Of course, she does. I paid." The old woman turned back, and the cast of her black eyes seemed more pity than anger. She grabbed Catherine's hand and stared at it for a moment more.

"You are going to the sea where a great evil waits."

Catherine wanted to laugh, but the intensity of the little woman wouldn't allow it.

"It hungers for your blood, hungers in a way you cannot understand. For it, death is too kind. Agony and pain are its desires, more pain than you can endure."

"Oh my god," Sheila said.

"Go on," Catherine forced through clenched teeth. "What else?"

"You cannot escape it. If you go, you will serve it with your dying scream."

"There must be a way to stop this 'evil'. What is it?"

Sheila grabbed Catherine's arm, but Catherine shook off her hand.

The Hag ran a black, gnarled fingernail along her palm, and Catherine shivered. "The spirit must be released. It must recover what is missing."

"What the hell does that mean?" Catherine said. "It does not matter."

The Hag dropped her hand. "You do not believe."

"That's enough!" Sheila thrust the pint into the Hag's hand. "Go! Go! Go!"

The Hag took the pint and stared into Catherine's eyes. Catherine couldn't find the courage to challenge. Then, the Hag drained the ale in one long pull, slamming the glass on the table when she was finished.

Without another word, the little creature limped away, leaving Sheila and Catherine speechless.

"What ho, Catherine!"

Catherine looked up as Nigel and Paul, two men from the Beeb arrived, pints in hand.

"Lord," Nigel said. "You look like you've seen a ghost."

"Worse," Sheila said. "The Hag just read her future."

"And predicted what? A long, running out of money in Europe?" Paul laughed.

Catherine forced a smile despite the cold in her heart. "OK, which one of you did it?"

"Did what?" Nigel asked.

"Paid that morbid creature to scare the pants off me."

"Not me," Nigel said.

"Nor me," Paul added.

"Right." Catherine turned to Sheila.

"Don't look at me. I may be dark, but I'm not that dark."

"OK, mates," Catherine said. "I never get mad, but I do get even." She grabbed her glass. "Woe betide the person responsible." She drained her glass and slammed it on the table.

Later, outside the pub, Catherine and Sheila hugged.

"I shouldn't have had that last pint," Sheila said.

"You don't have far to go."

"You'll email and text and skype, correct?"

"You'll get sick of me."

Sheila stepped back. "I know what the Hag said is silly, but you will be careful, won't you?" Catherine worked up her best smile.

She gave Sheila a warm smile. "I've travelled through some of the most dangerous places in the world. I don't think a village by the sea is going to do me in."

"I bet it was Nigel."

"What?"

"I bet Nigel paid off the Hag. It's like him."

"Nigel thinks I'm going to Paris."

"Why would he think that?"

"Because I didn't want him hunting me down over some nonsense detail."

"Ah, Paul then."

"Paul thinks I'm going to Paris too."

Sheila frowned and then burbled. "It wasn't me, Catho. I swear, it wasn't me."

"I believe you," Catherine said. "Go home."

With a wave, Sheila turned and weaved down the walk. Catherine turned away, a sense of dread lodged deep in her soul.

A little village by the sea. Nothing more.

The Haunting of Highcliff Hall

Available Now at

http://a-fwd.to/2Fsd7F6

Other Titles by Cat Knight

The Haunting of Elleric Lodge

Available here: http://a-fwd.to/6aa9u0N

The Haunting of Fairview House

Available here: http://a-fwd.to/6lKwbG1

The Haunting of Weaver House

Available here: http://a-fwd.to/7Do5KDi

The Haunting of Grayson House

Available here: http://a-fwd.to/3nu8fqk

The Haunting of Keira O'Connell

Available here: http://a-fwd.to/2qrTERv

The Haunting of Ferncoombe Manor

Available here: http://a-fwd.to/32MzXfz

The Haunting of Highcliff Hall

Available here: http://a-fwd.to/2Fsd7F6

The Haunting of Stone Street Cemetery

Available here: http://a-fwd.to/1txL6vk

About the Author

Cat Knight has been fascinated by fantasy and the paranormal since she was a child. Where others saw animals in clouds, Cat saw giants and spirits. A mossy rock was home to faeries, and laying beneath the earth another dimension existed. That was during the day. By night there were evil spirits lurking in the closet and under her bed. They whirled around her in the witching hour, daring her to come out from under her blanket and face them. She breathed in a whisper and never poked her head out from under her covers nor got up in the dark no matter how scared she was, because for sure, she would die at the hands of ghosts or demons. How she ever grew up without suffocating remains a mystery.

Never Miss A book

Subscribe to Cat Knight's newsletter for new release announcements

http://eepurl.com/cKReuz

Like me on Facebook

https://www.facebook.com/catknightauthor/

CAT KNIGHT

Printed in Great Britain
by Amazon